HEIDI HECKELBECK
Is a Flower Girl

By Wanda Coven
Illustrated by Priscilla Burris

LITTLE SIMON
New York London Toronto Sydney New Delhi

LITTLE SIMON
An imprint of Simon & Schuster Children's Publishing Division
1230 Avenue of the Americas, New York, New York 10020
Copyright © 2014 by Simon & Schuster, Inc.
All rights reserved, including the right of reproduction in whole or in part in any form.
LITTLE SIMON is a registered trademark of Simon & Schuster, Inc., and associated colophon is a trademark of Simon & Schuster, Inc.
For information about special discounts for bulk purchases, please contact Simon & Schuster Special Sales at 1-866-506-1949 or business@simonandschuster.com.
The Simon & Schuster Speakers Bureau can bring authors to your live event. For more information or to book an event contact the Simon & Schuster Speakers Bureau at 1-866-248-3049 or visit our website at www.simonspeakers.com.
Manufactured in the United States of America 0414 FFG
First Edition 10 9 8 7 6 5 4 3 2 1
Library of Congress Cataloging-in-Publication Data
Coven, Wanda.
Heidi Heckelbeck is a flower girl / by Wanda Coven ; illustrated by Priscilla Burris. — First edition.
pages cm. — (Heidi Heckelbeck ; 11)
Summary: Unlike her brother, Henry, who is excited to be the ring bearer in Aunt Sophie's wedding, Heidi is not looking forward to walking down the aisle in a fancy flower girl dress, but when Henry loses the ring, Heidi must stir up a spell to create a new one before the big day.
ISBN 978-1-4814-0498-3 (pbk : alk. paper) — ISBN 978-1-4814-0499-0 (hc : alk. paper) — ISBN 978-1-4814-0500-3 (ebook) [1. Witches—Fiction. 2. Weddings—Fiction. 3. Flower girls—Fiction.] I. Burris, Priscilla, illustrator. II. Title.
PZ7.C83393Hi 2014
[Fic]—dc23
2013037335

CONTENTS

Chapter 1

MISS HARRIET'S

Heidi Heckelbeck had a lot on her mind. She had been spying on Principal Pennypacker for more than a week because she was pretty sure he was a witch. Why else would he have a *Book of Spells* in his office? At least, that's what the book looked

like. Now she just had to prove he
was a witch. And on top of her witch
detective work, Heidi had also been
asked to be a flower girl in her aunt
Sophie's wedding.

Aunt Sophie was Dad's sister, and
soon she was going to marry Uncle
Ned in the Heckelbecks' backyard.

Well, Uncle Ned wasn't actually Heidi's uncle *yet*—not until after the wedding—but Heidi and Henry had called him Uncle Ned ever since he'd gotten engaged to Aunt Sophie. Now Heidi had to go dress shopping.

Ugh, thought Heidi as she stood in the middle of Miss Harriet's dress

shop. She had never shopped for
a fancy dress before. Now she was
surrounded by them. Miss Harriet
looked Heidi up and down. Then
she sifted through the dress racks
and pulled out dresses in a rainbow
of pastel colors: strawberry, mint
yellow, cream, and blue.

"You'll make an enchanting flower girl in any one of these," she said, holding the flouncy dresses in front of Heidi.

Heidi frowned. *I'll look like a poofy powder puff in any one of those dresses,* she thought. It wasn't that Heidi hated dresses. It's just that they weren't exactly her style. She was more of an everyday girl.

Heidi followed her mother into the dressing room.

Then she pulled off her favorite kitty cat top and jean skirt. Heidi left on her black-and-white-striped tights and sneakers. Then she slipped a strawberry dress over her head. Mom tied the satin sash around Heidi's waist. The dress had a scratchy skirt that stuck out like a giant lampshade.

"I feel like I'm caught in a big fishing net," complained Heidi. "And the skirt part is itchy."

"It's called crinoline," said Heidi's mom. "It's a very fancy dress material."

Heidi glanced in the mirror. "It looks like something Smell-a-nie would wear," she said.

Melanie Maplethorpe, also known as Smell-a-nie, was Heidi's worst enemy.

"Forget Melanie," said Mom. "That

dress is too pink
with your red hair.
Let's try another
one."

Heidi tried on
another dress,
and another
and another.

The mint dress
made her look like she hadn't slept
in a week. The yellow dress made her
look like a glass of lemonade. And
the cream dress made her look like
a miniature bride. Then Mom zipped
the blue dress and tied the sash.

Heidi looked in the mirror. She turned this way and that while she looked at herself.

"I love it," said Mom.

"'Love' is such a strong word," said Heidi.

"But it looks very good on you," said Mom.

Heidi scratched her neck. "The ruffles make me itch," she said.

"You will get used to them," said Mom. "You won't even realize they're there when you walk down the aisle."

"Merg," said Heidi.

"Beautiful," said Mom.

"Perfect!" exclaimed Miss Harriet.

"Except for the black-and-white-striped tights and sneakers."

Miss Harriet scurried into another room and came back with a pair of light blue ballet flats. She also brought Heidi a basket to hold her flower petals. Heidi had been told a flower girl had to sprinkle flower petals all along the wedding aisle.

Heidi slipped on the blue flats and stared at her feet. *Eww,* she thought as she wrinkled her nose.

Click! Miss Harriet snapped Heidi's picture.

"Perfect!" said Miss Harriet as she hurried to her computer to download the picture. "I'll give you a copy to take home."

The flash had made Heidi see spots. She rubbed her eyes. Then she stared at herself again in the mirror.

"Can I at least wear my blue-and-white-striped tights with this girly outfit?" asked Heidi.

"Sure," Mom said. "Be your own flower girl!"

And that made Heidi feel a teeny bit better.

Chapter 2

A BAD DREAM

Henry held a small sofa pillow in his hands like a tea tray. On top of the pillow sat a red ring pop. He walked slowly across the kitchen, being careful not to drop the ring pop.

"Look at me!" he cried. "I'm a RING BEAR!"

Heidi rolled her eyes.

"You mean a ring bear-ER," she said.

"Whatever," said Henry. He circled the kitchen table. "I get to carry the rings that Uncle Ned and Aunt Sophie give each other."

"Big whoop," said Heidi.

"I also get to wear a tuxedo," Henry added.

"Double big whoop," said Heidi.

"Your aunt Sophie's wedding *is* a very big whoop," Dad said.

"All I know is that I have to wear a froofy party dress," said Heidi.

"I can't wait to see THAT," said Henry.

"Merg," growled Heidi as she stomped out of the room.

That night Heidi had a bad dream about the wedding. In her dream, the skirt on her fancy party dress had grown enormous. The ruffles around her neck had climbed all the way up to her chin. Then she realized it was her turn to walk down the aisle. The guests all stared at her. Heidi tried

to bend over to pick up her basket of petals, but she couldn't. She tried again and tipped over. Heidi lay on her stomach, kicking her feet, like a bug in a swimming pool.

Then, *bing!* Just like that, she woke up, except she was still kicking. Heidi had gotten all twisted in her covers. Finally she wriggled free of the sheets and sighed in relief.

Later at school, Heidi told her friend Lucy Lancaster about the wedding and the flower girl dress.

"You're so lucky!" Lucy exclaimed. "I've always wanted to be in a wedding."

"Do you want to trade places?" asked Heidi.

23

"Very funny," said Lucy. "So, what's your dress look like?"

"I brought a picture," Heidi said. "But you have to promise not to laugh."

"Promise," said Lucy.

Heidi reached into her back pocket and pulled out the photo Miss Harriet

had taken in the store. She started to hand it to Lucy, but before Lucy got it, Melanie snatched it out of Heidi's hand.

"Let ME see!" cried Melanie.

"Hey, that's MINE!" cried Heidi.

Melanie looked at the picture and squealed with laughter.

"Oh my gosh," cried Smell-a-nie in between giggles. "That dress is SO icky!"

Stanley Stonewrecker snuck up behind Melanie and grabbed the photo out of her hand. Melanie kept right on laughing as Stanley looked at the picture.

"Wow, Heidi," said Stanley as he handed the picture back to Heidi. "You look great in that dress."

Melanie huffed in disgust.

Lucy peeked at the photo. "Stanley's right, you do look great," she said. "And PS, Melanie, if you think THAT dress is icky, you should get a whole new wardrobe."

Melanie folded her arms and turned up her nose.

"I'll bet Heidi won't even be able to walk in that dress," said Melanie. "She'll probably trip and fall when she walks down the aisle."

Heidi couldn't believe what Melanie had just said. It was as if she knew Heidi had had a bad dream about falling down at the wedding. *How does she do that?* Heidi thought. *And what if I really do fall down in front of everybody?*

It was too awful to think about.

Chapter 3

LILAC POWDER

On Saturday, Heidi helped Aunt Trudy clean out her basement. Aunt Trudy was Mom's sister, and she was also a witch. Aunt Trudy had the best castoffs. Heidi had gotten things like glass beads, jeweled charms, funky buttons, pressed flowers, and empty makeup containers. Cleaning at her aunt's house was like going on a treasure hunt.

Today, Aunt Trudy had a whole list of things for Heidi to do. She had her fold clothes for giveaway boxes, pack books for the library book drive, and clean shelves. On one shelf Heidi found a shoe box filled with seashells, sea glass, and dried starfish. She poked through the box.

"These shells are so pretty," Heidi said.

Aunt Trudy looked over her shoulder. "I collected them ages ago," she said. "Feel free to take them, or I'll put them in a giveaway box."

Heidi set the shoe box in her take-home pile. Then she got back to work. Heidi thought about the wedding as she dusted off a shelf.

"Aunt Trudy, have you ever been a flower girl?" she asked.

Aunt Trudy tossed a book into one of the boxes. "No," she said. "But I always dreamed of being one."

"You did?" questioned Heidi. "Why?"

"Because being a flower girl is a special honor," said Aunt Trudy. "And you also get to wear a fancy dress and walk down the aisle."

"Yuck," said Heidi. "That's the worst part, if you ask me."

"Don't you like to dress up?" asked Aunt Trudy.

"Well, sometimes," admitted Heidi. "I just don't like to be in the spotlight."

"Why not?" said Aunt Trudy.

"Because what if I trip and fall in front of all the guests?"

Aunt Trudy looked over the top of her glasses. "So what if you did?" she said. "It would make a good story."

"I just don't like it," said Heidi.

Aunt Trudy put her arm around her niece. "Being in the spotlight is

special," she said. "And your aunt
Sophie picked you to be her flower
girl because she loves you and thinks
you'll do a good job."

"I know," mumbled Heidi.

"Just pretend you're on a fashion show runway in Paris," Aunt Trudy said.

Heidi tried to picture herself on a runway in Paris. It actually sounded kind of fun.

Then her aunt picked up a pile of
old winter clothes and put them on
a card table in front of Heidi.

"Let's fold these and put them in a
shopping bag," Aunt Trudy said.

Heidi nodded and pulled a sweater

from the pile. Something fell onto the floor. It was a little satchel. *It must've been wrapped in the sweater,* thought Heidi. She picked up the satchel and undid the drawstring. The bag was filled with purple powder. Heidi sniffed the powder. *Ah-choo! Ah-choo! Ah-choo!*

"Bless you!" said Aunt Trudy. She gave Heidi a tissue, and then she began to laugh.

"What's so funny?" Heidi asked, wiping her nose.

"The lilac powder!" said Aunt Trudy. "Lilac powder makes witches sneeze."

"It does?"

"Yup, every time," Aunt Trudy said.

Heidi found this *very* interesting.

"Does it work on ALL witches?" she asked.

"Every last one."

Wow, Heidi thought. *I could use this lilac powder on Principal Pennypacker. If he sneezes, I'll know for sure he's a witch.*

"May I take this

45

satchel home?" Heidi asked.

"Sure," said Aunt Trudy as she began to sweep the floor. "I've got plenty of lilac powder."

Heidi stuffed the satchel into her pocket. She had forgotten all about being a flower girl. Now all she could think about was how to get Principal Pennypacker to smell the lilac powder.

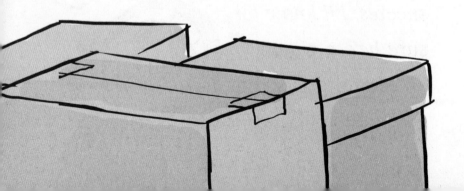

Chapter 4

FLOWER POWER

On Monday, Heidi spied on Principal Pennypacker at school. She hadn't figured out exactly how she was going to get him to sniff the powder, but she had to find a way. She sat on the school steps and watched the principal oversee the children at

drop-off. He waved and talked to the parents who had rolled down their car windows. *Hmm,* thought Heidi. *Drop-off is too busy. I'll have to find a better time.*

On the way to art class Heidi saw

Principal Pennypacker giving a tour to a mother and two children. Heidi remembered what it was like to be new. *I'm sure glad that's not me,* she thought.

Heidi paused at the water fountain,

and as she drank she kept an eye on the principal. He showed the family the student artwork hanging in the hallway. *I'll never get him to sniff the lilac powder when he's on a school tour,* she thought. Heidi wiped her mouth with the back of her hand and continued down the hall. Principal Pennypacker smiled as she passed by.

At lunch Heidi chose a seat near the faculty table. The principal sat at the head of the table. She watched him eat a slice of pizza. *If only I could sprinkle a little lilac powder on his pizza,* thought Heidi. But it would be way too obvious.

Lucy and Bruce Bickerson set their lunch trays down next to Heidi.

"So, how's the whole flower girl thing going?" asked Lucy.

"Same," said Heidi. "Mostly boring and pretty dumb."

Lucy laughed. "You're so funny," she said. "Most girls would give anything to be a flower girl."

Heidi shrugged and pulled the cheese off her pizza.

"Not me," she said.

At recess Heidi stood in line for foursquare and watched Principal Pennypacker. He was talking to her teacher, Mrs. Welli. *Darn,* thought Heidi. *He's always with somebody.* Then she

noticed a patch of dandelions on the playing field behind the principal and her teacher. This gave Heidi an idea.

She stepped out of line, ran to the field, and began to pick dandelions. Then she pulled the satchel of lilac powder from  her pocket. Heidi undid the string and sprinkled the powder on the top of the flowers. Then she skipped toward the

principal with her bouquet.

"Hello, Heidi," said the principal. "I hear you're going to be in a wedding this weekend. What fun!"

"Sort of," Heidi said. Then she

held the flowers out in sniffing range. "Would you like to smell my fresh-picked flowers?"

Principal Pennypacker leaned over.

"Why, I'd love to," he said.

He smelled the dandelions. Heidi waited for a big sneeze. But nothing

happened. She pulled the dandelions
out from under the principal's nose
and walked away. *That's weird,* she
thought. Heidi sniffed the dandelions
to see if the powder still worked.

Ah-choo! Ah-choo! Ah-choo!

Merg, thought Heidi as she tossed the dandelions into the bushes. *I guess Principal Pennypacker's not a witch after all.* She was a bit disappointed. It had been fun spying on him. *Oh well,* she thought, and ran back to the foursquare game.

Chapter 5

PiRATE BOOTY

Wedding talk was the only talk at the Heckelbeck house all week. On Friday a large van delivered tables, chairs, and a large white tent. On Saturday several people in matching aprons set the tables and cooked food in the Heckelbecks' kitchen. The wedding would begin at four o'clock that afternoon.

Soon it was time to get ready. Dad, Uncle Ned, and Henry got dressed in Henry's room. Heidi, Mom, Aunt Sophie, and Aunt Trudy got ready in Heidi's parents' bedroom. Mom clasped Aunt Sophie's pearl necklace. Aunt Trudy tied Heidi's sash and clipped a powder-blue flower in Heidi's hair.

"Hold still, missy!" said Aunt Trudy.

"But this dress is itching me!" said Heidi.

Heidi did her best to hold still. Then Henry burst into the bedroom in his tuxedo. He had a plastic sword in his hand and a black eye patch over his left eye.

"Ahoy, me hearties!" cried Henry as he jumped onto an ottoman and pretended to scan the horizon.

Heidi ignored Henry's behavior, but she studied his outfit.

"You look like a miniature man,"
she said.

Henry planted his fists on his hips.

"Methinks I am a well-dressed
pirate!" he said. "And my treasure
chest is chock-full of loot."

"What kind of loot?" asked Heidi. "It better not be anything from my room."

"Sparkling jewels and dazzling gems!" shouted Henry. "And today I added a very valuable ring to my treasure."

Heidi had a funny feeling. She knew what kind of ring Henry had added to his loot. She ran across the room, grabbed Henry by the arm, and dragged him into the hall.

"Do you have Aunt Sophie's wedding ring?" asked Heidi.

"Of course!" said Henry. "I'm the RING BEAR!"

"The ring bear-ER," Heidi corrected. "Now, where is it?"

"What?" asked Henry.

"The RING!"

"It's in my treasure chest!" Henry said.

"Does Uncle Ned know you have it?"

"No," Henry admitted.

"Well, you better give it back," said Heidi.

"But Dad gave it to me!" argued Henry.

"I don't care if Dad gave it to you.

Get it NOW," said Heidi. "If Uncle Ned doesn't have the ring, he and Aunt Sophie won't be able to get married."

"Oh no!" said Henry. "Will you help me look for it?"

Heidi let out a heavy sigh. "Come on," she said. "We haven't got much time before the wedding begins."

Chapter 6

WHAT IF?

Henry flipped open the skull latch on his wooden pirate chest and emptied the contents onto the playroom floor. Heidi and Henry combed through the silver and gold plastic coins and beaded necklaces. Heidi spied a fake ring and a plastic hotdog in the pile, but there wasn't a wedding ring.

"I can't believe you really lost the ring," Heidi said.

"I didn't mean to," said Henry.

"Maybe it's in the toy chest," suggested Heidi.

She ran to the toy chest and flung open the lid. Then she began to toss puppets, dodge balls, and plastic army men over her shoulder. Henry found a kaleidoscope. He peeked in the lens and twisted the end of it.

Heidi glared at Henry. "Put that down!" she shouted. "Don't you know that you're in HUGE trouble?"

Henry dropped the kaleidoscope and began searching through the trunk. But there was no ring.

Heidi tipped over a tub full of sports equipment. Super Balls and tennis balls rolled across the floor.

"What if we don't find the ring?" asked Henry.

"Then there really won't be a wedding," said Heidi.

"And if there isn't a wedding, then what?"

"Then I won't have to wear this dumb dress," said Heidi.

"Hey, that's mean," Henry said.

"Besides, you look kind of pretty in that dress."

Heidi stopped searching and looked at her brother. "Thanks, little man," she said.

Then they carefully sorted through the sports equipment on the floor, but they still didn't find the ring.

They looked upstairs, downstairs, and under all the sofas and chairs. But the wedding ring was nowhere to be found.

"Let's face it," said Henry. "I'm dead."

"Pretty much," Heidi said. "But I have an idea."

RAZZLE-DAZZLE

"What's your idea?" asked Henry hopefully.

"Follow me," Heidi said.

They zoomed down the hall to Heidi's room.

"Shut the door," said Heidi.

Henry closed the door behind

them. Then Heidi knelt on the floor and pulled her *Book of Spells* and her Witches of Westwick medallion from under the bed.

"It's a good thing I'm a witch," said Heidi.

"You're not kidding," said Henry.

Heidi ran her finger down the Contents page and found the chapter called "Jewelry." She flipped through the pages to a spell called "Ring Replacer."

"What does it say?" Henry asked.

Heidi read the spell out loud.

*Has your favorite ring
fallen down the drain?
Perhaps you're a ring bearer
in a wedding and you have
no ring to bear? If you're
a witch in need of a ring,
then the Ring Replacer
is the spell for you!*

Henry pumped his fist. "I'm SAVED!" he cried.

"You're not saved yet," said Heidi as she looked at her clock radio. "The wedding starts in thirty minutes."

Heidi read the spell ingredients and directions out loud. "One paper clip, one teaspoon of sugar, one rhinestone. Mix the ingredients together in a bowl. Hold your Witches of Westwick medallion in one hand. Place your other hand over the mix and chant the following words: 'Razzle-dazzle, bling, bling,

bling—turn this mix into a ring!'"

Heidi put down the *Book of Spells*.

"Get a paper clip from my desk,"
said Heidi.

"Okay," said Henry.

"I'm going to get the sugar and
the rhinestone. Be right back!"

Heidi raced downstairs. She quickly
measured a teaspoon of sugar and
placed it in a small bowl. Then she
ran back to her room and opened
her dresser drawer. She pulled out

her DANCE DIVA T-shirt
and picked off a pink
rhinestone. Then she
dropped the rhine-
stone into the bowl.

Henry added the paper clip.

"We're all ready," said Heidi.

She slipped the medallion around her neck and held it in one hand. She placed her other hand over the mix and chanted the spell. Heidi uncovered the bowl, and they both looked inside. A ring with a huge pink stone in a clawlike setting sat at the bottom of the bowl. Heidi picked it up.

"Whoa," she said. "It's big."

"And bold," added Henry.

"And all wrong," declared Heidi. "It doesn't look anything like Aunt Sophie's wedding ring."

"NOW what are we going to do?" asked Henry.

"There's only one thing left TO do," Heidi said.

"What?" Henry asked.

"Fess up," said Heidi.

Chapter 8

THE REAL THING

Heidi pushed Henry into his bedroom. She watched from the door to see what would happen. Uncle Ned smiled at Henry and did a deep knee bend in his tuxedo. Dad tied his bow tie.

"Ready to roll?" asked Dad. "We

have to be in our places in fifteen minutes."

Henry stood still in front of Dad.

"Is something the matter?" asked Dad.

Henry looked at the floor. "Well, sort of," he began. "It's about Aunt Sophie's ring."

"The ring!" exclaimed Dad. "I almost forgot." Then he reached into his pocket and pulled out Aunt Sophie's ring!

Henry's jaw dropped. "Where did you find it?"

"Nowhere," said Dad. "I've had it all along."

Henry blinked in disbelief.
"You didn't think I'd give you the *real* ring?" asked Dad with a wink.

"It wasn't real?" Henry asked.

"No," said Dad. "It was just for practice. Now let's get your ring pillow ready."

Henry grabbed the ring pillow from on top of his dresser. Then Dad snapped the ring in place. Uncle Ned

attached his wedding band beside it.

"Can you take care of the *real* rings until we exchange vows?" asked Uncle Ned.

"Definitely!" said Henry. "And I promise not to take my eyes off them!"

"Great! Then let's have ourselves a wedding!" said Dad.

Chapter 9

A LiTTLE PRiNCESS

Heidi stepped into the backyard and gasped. At one end of the yard stood a white garden archway swirled with pale pink roses. White folding chairs had been set up in rows in front of the archway, with a path down the middle.

Two of Heidi's cousins played guitars as the guests took their seats. On another side of the yard were tables decorated with white linens, daisies, and votive candles. White paper lanterns had been strung from the tree branches. Next to the tables was a great white tent with tables, a dance floor, and a live band.

Wow, thought Heidi. *This looks like something out of a fairy tale!* Then it dawned on her. *That must be why I'm dressed like a princess!* Heidi felt a tingle of wedding magic.

"Here," said Mom, handing Heidi her flower girl basket.

Heidi lifted the basket to her nose. *Mmm,* she thought. *The roses smell so sweet!* Then she took her place next to Henry, who held his ring pillow proudly.

When the guests had all been seated, the wedding music began. Henry went down the aisle first.

"Good luck!" Heidi whispered.

"You too!" Henry whispered back before walking down the aisle.

Heidi followed behind Henry. She felt beautiful as she tossed the petals all along the aisle. All the guests smiled at Heidi, and she smiled back. *Being in the spotlight isn't so bad,* Heidi thought. Then the wedding

march began. Aunt Sophie walked
down the aisle. She held a bouquet of
freshly cut white roses in her hands.
She took her place next to Uncle Ned.

The bride and groom exchanged wedding vows and rings. Then they kissed.

"Eww!" Henry said a little too loudly.

Everyone laughed and clapped for the bride and groom.

Then the party began. Heidi and Henry danced on the lawn. They ate grilled chicken, hamburgers, and a double-fudge cake with vanilla cream-cheese frosting. Everyone laughed and clapped again when Henry caught the bride's bouquet.

Later on Heidi and Henry blew bubbles at Aunt Sophie and Uncle Ned as they left for their honeymoon.

Heidi sighed dreamily. "I love weddings," she said.

"What?" questioned Henry. "But I thought you HATED weddings."

"Not anymore," said Heidi.

Chapter 10

HARVEST MOON

The next day Heidi and Aunt Trudy went to Harvest Moon to buy some ingredients for Aunt Trudy's brews. Harvest Moon had regular grocery store items, but they also sold hard-to-find products that witches used in brews. Heidi got a shopping cart and steered it into the store.

"So, how did you like being a flower girl?" asked Aunt Trudy as she pulled out her shopping list.

"It was so much better than I thought," Heidi said. "I actually had a great time."

"Wow," said Aunt Trudy. "What changed your thinking?"

Heidi shrugged. "I dunno," she said. "It was different from what I expected."

"How so?" asked Aunt Trudy.

"Well, I thought it was going to be embarrassing to wear a fancy dress and

walk down the aisle in front of that many people. But it wasn't. It was completely magical."

Aunt Trudy smiled.

"I thought it was magical too. I'm so glad you had a good time."

"Me too," agreed Heidi. "I had the wrong idea about flower girls."

"Well, sometimes things are not always what we expect," Aunt Trudy said.

"No kidding," said Heidi.

They high-fived. Then Aunt Trudy pulled a jar of bee pollen from the shelf and placed it into the cart. She checked her list.

"Heidi, would you find the bay leaves?" she asked. "I'll get the pickled ginger. Then we can meet at the checkout line."

"Sure," said Heidi.

Heidi walked down a few rows and found the spice aisle. When she was partway down she saw a man duck around the corner into the next aisle.

He was bald except for a tuft of hair above each ear.

Hey! thought Heidi. *Is that Principal Pennypacker?* She ran down the aisle and peeked around the corner. But when she looked, he was gone. *That's weird. It must've just been my imagination.*

Or was it?

Check out the next book starring

HEIDI HECKELBECK

If only I could get rid of this stupid cold, thought Heidi, then I could go to the festival. She flopped onto her bed. It could take days to get better, and by then the festival will be long gone. Heidi threw her stuffed owl against the wall. It bounced off and rolled under her dust ruffle. She reached over to pick it up and noticed her

An excerpt from *Heidi Heckelbeck Gets the Sniffles*

Check out the next book starring

HEIDI HECKELBECK

If only I could get rid of this stupid cold, thought Heidi, then I could go to the festival. She flopped onto her bed. It could take days to get better, and by then the festival will be long gone. Heidi threw her stuffed owl against the wall. It bounced off and rolled under her dust ruffle. She reached over to pick it up and noticed her

An excerpt from *Heidi Heckelbeck Gets the Sniffles*

Book of Spells under the bed. *Wait a second,* she thought. *Maybe I CAN get better faster.* She pulled the book out.

"There has to be a spell to cure a cold," she said to herself.

Heidi looked at the Contents page and found a whole chapter on health. There were remedies for everything from rashes to back pain. Then she found a spell called "No More Sickness!"

"Bingo!" said Heidi as she began to read the spell.

Do you have an upset stomach? Are you the

kind of witch who has a tendency to get tonsillitis? Or perhaps you've just come down with a rotten cold. If anything ails you, then this is the spell for you!

The mix of ingredients sounded one hundred percent disgusting, but it wasn't as bad as feeling sick. Heidi bookmarked the page. Then she slid into her fuzzy blue bunny slippers and headed downstairs. She paused on the bottom stair and listened. Mom was on the phone. Heidi tiptoed past her office and into the kitchen. . . .

An excerpt from *Heidi Heckelbeck Gets the Sniffles*